A LIFT-THE-FLAP BOOK

CORDUROY

goes to the

FIRE STATION

BASED ON THE CHARACTER CREATED BY DON FREEMAN
STORY BY B. G. HENNESSY • PICTURES BY LISA McCUE

VIKING

Today, Corduroy's class is visiting the fire station.
The hook and ladder truck is parked outside. The ladders
help the firefighters rescue people on roofs or up in high
buildings. The hooks pull down burning ceilings so the
water from the hoses can reach the fire.

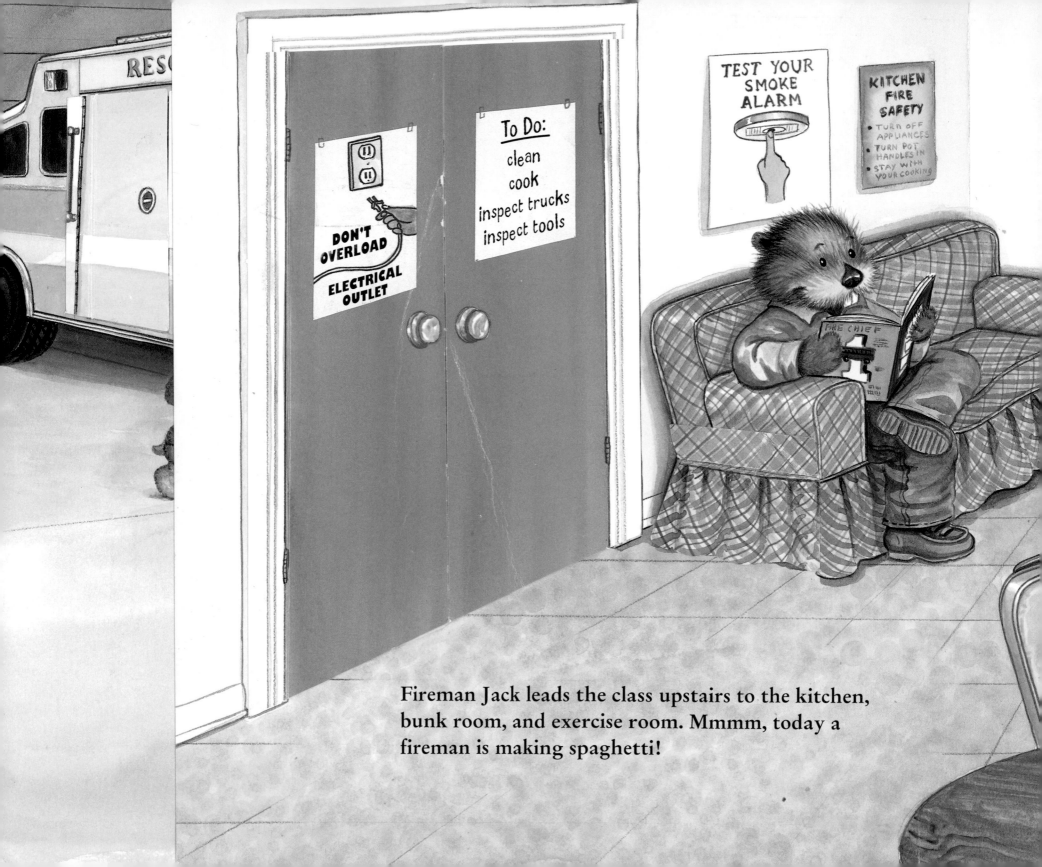

RESC

DON'T OVERLOAD
ELECTRICAL OUTLET

To Do:
clean
cook
inspect trucks
inspect tools

TEST YOUR SMOKE ALARM

KITCHEN FIRE SAFETY
• TURN OFF APPLIANCES
• TURN POT HANDLES IN
• STAY WITH YOUR COOKING

FIRE CHIEF

Fireman Jack leads the class upstairs to the kitchen,
bunk room, and exercise room. Mmmm, today a
fireman is making spaghetti!

KITCHEN TIPS

- Never leave cooking unattended
- Keep appliances clean

Fireman Jack tells the class never to play with fire or matches.
If their clothes ever do catch on fire he tells them:
DON'T RUN. STOP, DROP, AND ROLL. That will help put
out the flames. The class practices. Good rolling, Corduroy.

He shows them the special clothes firefighters wear.
Everything is very heavy. It has to be to protect the
firefighter from the fire, heat, and smoke. The firefighters
keep their clothes downstairs near the fire trucks, ready
to go. Everybody in the class gets a junior fireman's hat.

Downstairs, the firefighters are checking the trucks.
They test the lights and sirens. Cover your ears,
Corduroy! The class helps clean the headlights.
Then the firefighters have a surprise!

Corduroy's class is going to ride a fire truck in a parade!

You'd make a good firefighter, Corduroy!

DON FREEMAN was born in San Diego, California, and moved to New York City to study art, making his living as a jazz trumpeter. Following the loss of his trumpet on a subway train, Mr. Freeman turned his talents to art full-time. In the 1940s, he began writing and illustrating children's books. His many popular titles include *Corduroy*, *A Pocket for Corduroy*, *Beady Bear*, *Dandelion*, *Bearymore*, and *Norman the Doorman*.

LISA McCUE has illustrated more than eighty books, including *Corduroy's Halloween*, *Corduroy's Easter*, *Corduroy's Christmas*, and *Corduroy's Birthday*. She lives in Annapolis, Maryland, with her husband and their two sons.

A bear's share of the royalties from *Corduroy Goes to the Fire Station* goes to the Don and Lydia Freeman Research Fund to support psychological care and research concerning children with life-threatening illness.

Thanks to the Eastport Fire Station in Annapolis, Maryland, the Annapolis Fire Department in Maryland, and Fire Station 814 in Scottsdale, Arizona, for help with this book.

VIKING
Published by the Penguin Group
Penguin Putnam Books for Young Readers, 345 Hudson Street, New York, New York 10014, U.S.A.
Penguin Books Ltd, 80 Strand, London WC2R 0RL, England
Penguin Books Australia Ltd, 250 Camberwell Road, Camberwell, Victoria 3124, Australia
Penguin Books Canada Ltd, 10 Alcorn Avenue, Toronto, Ontario, Canada M4V 3B2
Penguin Books (N.Z.) Ltd, 182-190 Wairau Road, Auckland 10, New Zealand

Penguin Books Ltd, Registered Offices: Harmondsworth, Middlesex, England

First published in 2003 by Viking, a division of Penguin Putnam Books for Young Readers.

3 5 7 9 10 8 6 4

Text copyright © Penguin Putnam Inc., 2003
Illustrations copyright © Lisa McCue, 2003
All rights reserved

ISBN: 0-670-03600-5

Printed in Malaysia
Set in Stempel Garamond